Sophie Wo...
about Eucharist

Debby Bradley

Illustrated by
Lula Guzmán

Liguori
LIGUORI, MISSOURI

Dedication

Grateful
for love and support from my husband, Bill,
and children, Claire Marie, Teman John Kaiser,
and Molly Renee.

Blessed
to have as my first religious examples
Fr. Bill Vos and Ade Ledermann.

Thankful
to have witnessed the inspiration of these who have
joined the communion of saints: Kenneth Besetzny,
Judith Batton, Helen Marais, and John Kaiser.

Imprimi Potest:
Harry Grile, CSsR, Provincial
Denver Province, The Redemptorists

Published by Liguori Publications
Liguori, Missouri 63057

To order, call 800-325-9521
www.liguori.org

p ISBN: 978-0-7648-2339-8
e ISBN: 978-0-7648-6868-9

Liguori Publications, a nonprofit corporation, is an apostolate of The Redemptorists.
To learn more about The Redemptorists, visit Redemptorists.com.

Printed in the United States of America
17 16 15 14 13 / 5 4 3 2 1
First Edition

There once was a little girl.
Her name was Sophie.
Sophie wondered about many things.

Sophie liked going to church. She liked the singing, she liked seeing her friends, and she liked praying for people.

One day Sophie wondered about something she sees people do at Mass.

She asked her mommy,
"Why do big people eat that round
white thing and drink from that cup?"

Mommy asked, "You know how we love
to tell stories about Jesus?"

Sophie nodded.

"We do that because Jesus was so great, and we want to remember him.

"Before Jesus died, he ate a special meal with his friends.

"Jesus didn't want his friends to forget him and all the lessons he'd taught them.

"He asked his friends to eat that special meal of bread and wine again and again after he was gone.

"He said they should think about him each time they did it.

"Jesus said he'd be inside the bread and wine, and then inside us!

"Jesus' friends didn't want to forget him, so they promised to have the special meal again and again.

"We call this special meal *Eucharist*,
a word that means "thanksgiving."
Sometimes Eucharist is also called
Communion.

"Today, we do two things
to remember Jesus:
First, we eat the
round, white **host**.

"Next, we drink
a sip of wine
from a special cup
called a **chalice**."

23

Sophie thought for a minute.
Then she asked, "May I have Jesus
in this special way?"

"Yes, when you're older and you've learned more about it," said Mommy.

"I can't wait to take the host and wine to remember Jesus!" Sophie said happily.

Sophie felt very grown up, because now she understood Eucharist.

Sophie Wonders
About the Sacraments